JULIA BOPS TO THE BEAT

Researched and written by **Felisha Bradshaw** (PB&j)
Illustration by Aveira Studio
Graphic Touches by Raymundo Osio

For permission requests, please contact:
BNHM.Publishing@gmail.com

Printed in the United States.

This book belongs to:

_____

Can I Read It?

Is this book easy, too hard or just right?
Use your fingers!

Go to the middle of this book and choose a page, then start reading.
For every word you do not know, count one finger on your hand. Look at the
guides below and see if the book is right for you.

If you counted:

1. Finger: easy!
2. Fingers: just right!
3. Fingers: a little hard, but fun to try.
4. Fingers: Difficult. (Read with a parent or a friend)
5. Fingers: Too had for now. (Save it for later)

YELLOW	PURPLE
Beginners	Ready For Longer Sentences

NOTE TO PARENTS
READING A LOUD WITH YOUR CHILD

Research shows that being involved and reading aloud to children is vital in encouraging them to read. Getting a head start in language and literacy skills and better prepared for school, depends on how much support is given and it starts with US!

- Be silly! Do voice-overs! Get into character! The more interactive you are the more active they will want to be.

- As you read along, trace your fingers under the words to familiarize them with the reading process. We want them to know words make up the story.

- Leave time to go over the pictures. Point out certain things in the story that stress the story line so, it doesn't break the concentration of the story's theme.

- Link up the events in the book to their real life events.

- Answer questions along the way. It can serve as away into their thoughts (way of thinking, their thinking process).

- When the child is reading aloud and isn't sure about a word's pronunciation give it to them immediately so they don't lose focus on the reading itself.

- If the child is in the process of sounding out the words let them feel it out first.

- If you hear a word pronounced wrong, like moose for mouse; have your child re-read. They may very well catch their mistake. If not show the difference in sound.

I truly hope this helps. After doing extensive reading research on the web, I found these points and I wanted to share them with our readers.

For the Love of Reading,

PB&j

Dear Parents,

Through Brand New Happy Moon Publishing, our little readers are developing a love for reading. When you read to them and with them, they soon will read to themselves and to you out loud. Brand New Happy Moon Publishing opens new worlds, expanding our little reader's imag ination through each page, each colorful scene and memorable characters.

In the Julia Grows and Knows Series the lesson addressed is "growing". Julia is learning as our little readers are learning and they are growing and gaining a greater perspective of their own challenges and experiences.

Thank you for allowing your children to be our little readers and to see life through Julia's eyes.

PB&j

I, _____

(your name)

have read this book

☐ once

☐ twice

☐ again and again

Inspired By:

Julia Bradshaw (Auntie's most beautiful princess)

John Merced

In Memory of the Children with Wings:

Sincere Pettway

Written for the Brilliant Minds of:

Julia Bradshaw
Jada Skyy Williams
Bali
Kamiyah & Baby Max
Madison Charlton

This book is dedicated to:

Syari and Harmony Joyner
Bali and Cyrus
CJ Donan Osio

After an early morning rise and the day comes to... Julia imagines a world of drums and hums, rump-a-bump-bums and sometimes musical beats that never go undone.

Every morning she jumps out of bed with the tunes playing in her head. Julia hears a certain thump, thump, thump as she jumps, jumps, jumps and hops, hops, hops as she bops, bops, bops to the beat.

Julia doesn't understand why Mom can't hear
the boom, boom, boom from the musical tunes
that keep Julia's fingers tap, tap, tapping,
snap, snap, snapping while she's rapping
to the beat in her room.

Julia's hands are waving wildly and
her feet are kicking out side to side.
There is nothing that can
break her stride.

Even though her shadow is big on
the wall, she still remains small, skipping and
flipping down the hall as she glides.

She passes her two brothers, Jake and Jay.
But they shake their heads and point, laugh and
say, "Julia still hears baby voices in her head."
"She ain't nothing like us! We are big boys.
We play with big boy toys instead."

Jake and Jay tossed the ball over Julia and traveled down the hall. But, that didn't stop lil' Julia at all! They couldn't hear because she wasn't ready to speak.

She spoke and lived through sounds and pounds, snaps and taps, raps and beats.

Julia heads for the bathroom to brush
her teeth, then back to her room to gather
her stuff. She has her own way of doing
things as the sounds sing, "Huffity, huff, huff!

Clunk Clunk Clunk! Tweedle leedle leet!" Julia
bounced and pounced like someone
was tickling her feet.

"Julia, Jake and Jay! Let's go! What did I say?"
Mom watches as her children scurry to the car.
Jake and Jay run past Julia, but they don't get
very far. "Do you have all the things you need
for school?" Jake and Jay give each other high
five, "Of course mom, boys rule!"

Julia ignores the boys and repeats as she bops, hops and trots to the beat. Now Julia's bopping to the beat from her car seat. Even though, Jake and Jay are doing their own thing. They can't help but bop non-stop and sing.

Julia's mom smiles, because for a while, she was watching her children through the rear view mirror. What tickled Mom the most was they claimed to be too big to hear her.

"That's outrageous, there's no way Julia's bopping to the beat is contagious," Mom said, as she too began bopping her head.

But, there was something about the way Julia didn't speak or didn't say it. Instead, from beginning to end; inside her head sounds all around replay it.

They formed their own words, giving everything meaning; every boom and every bang. Like the sound, pots made when they touched; clang clang!

She knew then it meant dinner was being prepared. Funny how this all made sense, just by the things she'd hear.

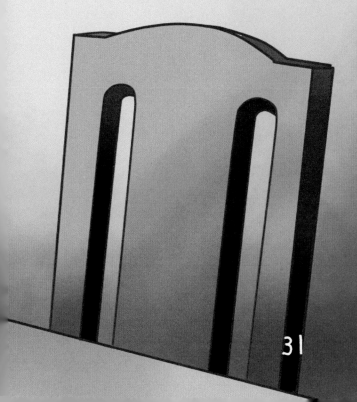

So, it didn't matter how much her big brothers teased, she loved how sounds flow.

What they didn't know is that she took sounds from all around and everywhere they'd go. The thump, thump, thump is the sound from the basketball Jake dribbled fast and slow.

The tapping and snapping that has Julia rapping can be easily heard. It's the tunes that soon will become Julia's first words.

Sounds slip from Julia's lips, for the first time. There was no boom, boom, booms, snaps or taps nor did she need the rhythm and rhymes. She now sounded out words not beats. But, it was the sounds around first, that taught her to speak!

THE END

THE HUGGING MONSTER

"It has bubble eyes, green and purple feet
large, fluffy and furry."

Join Julia as she conqures her fear.

"Comes with Coloring Book"

www.brandnewhappymoonpublishing.com

Made in the USA
Middletown, DE
04 June 2022

66585572R00024